'I've thought very hard about it,' the headmaster smiled, 'and I've decided to pick you for your first match in goal for us.'

Chris tried to say something, but his throat tightened and he remained speechless.

'Congratulations! You're a very promising goalie, and I know you won't let us down.'

For Chris Weston, several years younger than the rest of the school team, this is his big chance to prove his skills in goal. And this is no ordinary match either – but a vital Cup-tie against Shenby School, his school's main rivals!

Rob Childs is a Leicestershire teacher with many years experience of coaching and organizing school and area representative sports teams.

The Big Match

The Big Match

Rob Childs
Illustrated by Tim Marwood

YOUNG CORGI BOOKS

JF

THE BIG MATCH
A YOUNG CORGI BOOK 0 552 52451 4

Originally published in Great Britain by
Young Corgi Books

PRINTING HISTORY
Young Corgi edition published 1987
Reprinted 1987, 1988 (twice), 1990, 1991, 1992

7434
─────
2 34

This book is set in 14/18 pt Century Schoolbook
by Colset Private Limited, Singapore

Young Corgi Books are published by Transworld Publishers
Ltd., 61–63 Uxbridge Road, Ealing, London W5 5SA, in
Australia by Transworld Publishers (Australia) Pty. Ltd.,
15–25 Helles Avenue, Moorebank, NSW 2170, and in New
Zealand by Transworld Publishers (N.Z.) Ltd., 3 William
Pickering Drive, Albany, Auckland.

Printed and bound in Great Britain by
Cox & Wyman Ltd., Reading, Berks.

For my own Grandad, and those like him, with thanks for all their sporting encouragement to youngsters.

1 *Lost Ball*

'Great save, Chris!' shouted Andrew as his younger brother pushed yet another of his best shots round the post. 'You're unbeatable today.'

That was praise indeed from someone who played in the school football team.

Christopher Weston grinned and lay stretched out on the back garden lawn, posing for imaginary sports photographers. He wanted nothing more than to be in the Danebridge

Primary School team like Andrew was. He dreamed about it almost every night — and day-dreamed in class too, if his teacher let him.

He kept telling himself that his own chance to play would come soon. But really he knew he was going to have to wait, somehow, until he was a bit older.

Not that he wanted to be just an ordinary defender like his brother. No! Chris's single aim in life was to wear the special green goalkeeper's jersey with the large black number 1 stitched on the back.

Suddenly he jolted up. Andrew had quickly fetched the ball and was juggling it in the air, setting himself up for the shot as it fell.

He was already screaming,

'GOAL!' as Chris leapt and punched it high over the crossbar. The excited cries died in dismay as they watched the ball clip the top of the fence and flop out of sight into the neighbouring garden.

'Oh, no! That does it,' Andrew groaned, glaring. 'Now look what you've gone and done.'

'It wasn't my fault. Why blame me?' Chris complained in return. 'It's usually you who blasts it next door.'

Andrew went into a sulk. 'That was heading straight for the top corner. A goal all the way.'

'Until I fisted it!' Chris added, cheekily.

His brother sighed. 'Why do you have to be so good in goal?'

It was said in frustration, but he could not have paid Chris a better compliment. He loved keeping goal and wasn't interested in playing in any other position. Their grandad always said that he was a born goalie, and Chris was determined to prove him right.

Andrew continued to grumble.

'I bet it's landed right in the middle of the witch's flower-bed. She'll never let us have it back again.'

The 'witch' in question was old Mrs Witchell. She lived by herself now, a frail, wrinkled lady with a quick temper and rarely a good word for noisy young boys. They were generally careful not to cross her — especially near Hallowe'en time.

'She'll be hopping mad,' he went on, gloomily. 'Remember, she threatened

13

last time to have our football banned in the garden if it happened again.'

'She can't do that!' Chris gasped, horrified. 'Can she?'

They gazed with renewed pride at the small wooden goal they had clumsily nailed together during the summer; in their eyes it would have graced Wembley Stadium itself.

'We've got to do something,' declared Andrew in desperation.

'Like what? Please, dear little, old witchy, please may we have our ball back?' Chris mocked.

'Don't be stupid. No, we'll just have to sneak in and grab it before she notices.'

'Oh, yeah! Just like that. She might be lying in wait . . . and put a spell on us!'

Chris could already feel his heart-beat increasing at the mere thought of all the risks involved.

'Pooh! You are a baby sometimes, little brother Christopher. You're chicken!'

'No, I'm not.' He hated being called by his full name and knew it was only used to taunt him at times like this.

'Okay, let's go then,' Andrew challenged, and pushed him towards the gate before he could resist. He would never have admitted it to Chris, of course, but he didn't fancy raiding the witch's garden all by himself.

'Hold on, hold on!' Chris managed to blurt out. 'We can't just walk straight in there.'

'No, you're right,' Andrew considered. 'We must have a plan. This is going to need split-second timing ...'

So it was that, five minutes later, Chris found himself timidly tapping at Mrs Witchell's green front door.

His part in their tactics, as far as he understood, was to create a diversion

16

while Andrew sneaked round the back to get the ball. Right now, however, his older and wiser brother was crouching low behind the hedge, waiting for the moment either to advance or retreat.

At last the door slowly creaked open and the old woman's crinkly face creased up even more as she frowned when she saw who had disturbed her afternoon nap.

'Hmm . . . yes?' she demanded icily. 'What is it, boy? Speak up.'

For several seconds Chris lost his nerve and also his tongue, but then garbled out their story about collecting for the school jumble sale. He began to lose what little faith he had in the plan as he heard the words tumble out of his mouth, and he tailed off lamely, ' . . . er . . . anything would do . . . '

He started to back away under Mrs Witchell's hard, suspicious stare. She appeared to be about to shoo him off when her expression suddenly changed.

'Hmm ... wait a minute, not so fast. There is something. I've been meaning to get rid of them for ages. Stay where you are while I go and fetch them. Don't move.'

Chris was by now so terrified, he didn't think he could move his feet anyway.

She closed the door and immediately Andrew raced up the short path past him, ducking under the side window on his way to the back garden.

His luck was in. There was the white plastic ball nestling beneath a

18

small shrub on the flower border. He just had to pray that she would be too busy searching to glance out of the window and spot him.

Holding his breath, he slipped along the edge of the neatly-mown lawn and stepped carefully between the plants. 'Good,' he thought, 'no damage done.'

He grabbed his prize and clutched it tightly to his chest, then turned and fled back, throwing caution now to the wind. His heart was pounding the blood deafeningly into his ears in fear and excitement as he saw Chris frantically signalling that the coast was still clear.

Without checking, he ran full tilt past the house and didn't stop until he reached the safety of their own garden. He collapsed into the goalmouth, hugging himself and the ball with equal delight.

Chris felt awfully tempted to follow him, but somehow steeled himself to stay and see it through to the end. There was, in fact, to be a jumble sale shortly, so he decided he might as well get something for it after all his trouble.

But their plan had only just succeeded. No sooner had Andrew scampered out of sight when Mrs Witchell loomed over Chris again.

'What's the matter with you, boy? You look scared to death.'

'Nothing, Mrs Witch — ell.'

He almost forgot to add on the ending to her name.

'Hmm ... ' she murmured again through closed lips. 'Well, here you are. Have these, and don't come back

21

pestering me for more.'

Chris stammered some thanks and gratefully hurried out of her clutches, arriving back almost trembling with relief.

'We did it! We did it!' whooped Andrew. 'We tricked the old witch and got away with it.'

'We also got these.' Chris held out a pair of frayed, brown gloves for inspection. 'Just right for the jumble.'

They laughed and re-lived their daring raid. Chris even tried the gloves on in an act of bravado.

'Hey! They fit me as well.'

'C'mon, stop messing about now. Take them off and get back in goal.'

Andrew was still so pleased with himself that he took a huge swing at the ball for his first shot and its speed and power took Chris completely by surprise. He didn't even make a move for it. He could only watch it smack against the top of the bar and loop up high into the air at a crazy angle.

In horror and disbelief, they saw it sail right over the fence and disappear into that same forbidden garden again.

'Oh no!' they chorused, and both sank to their knees to listen for any sound.

Silence.

'Er ... I suppose we could try it again,' suggested Andrew, with a sheepish grin.

Chris exploded. 'No chance! You have got to be joking! I'm not going through all that a second time for anything.'

That was one ball, sadly, they never did see again.

2 Great News

'Christopher Weston!'

The sudden announcement of his own name startled him out of a day-dream.

'Stay behind after this assembly to see me,' continued Mr Jones, the headmaster of Danebridge Primary School, before moving on to appeal for more jumble to be brought in for the sale.

Chris felt himself going bright red as many eyes burned into him. To avoid them, he turned his head round to pick out Andrew who was sitting several rows behind him among the top juniors. All he received was an unsympathetic shrug of the shoulders.

He sighed. More trouble, no doubt, but he couldn't think what or why. Then his blood ran cold.

The old witch!

He supposed she must have discovered their trick and complained — and she hadn't seen Andrew, of course. Chris groaned to himself. He would probably be accused of stealing the stupid gloves or something. He had forgotten to bring them into school so there was not even any proof of his good intentions.

The others rose to leave the hall and

he braced himself. Whatever happened, he decided, he would not tell tales on Andrew. But even so, he wished they were walking into Mr Jones's office together.

'Close the door, Christopher, please.'

Before the headmaster could say anything else, Chris blurted out. 'I'm sorry, Mr Jones.'

He looked surprised. 'Sorry? What about?'

Chris hesitated, a little in doubt.

'For whatever I've done.'

Mr Jones laughed out loud, so much so that even Chris realized he must have misread the situation.

'You seem to have a guilty conscience about something, my boy, but we won't go into that just now.

I'm not telling you off, don't worry.
Quite the opposite, in fact.'

He paused to make sure he had the
boy's full attention.

'I've got some excellent news for
you. Something I know you've been
longing to hear.'

Chris was now even more puzzled
than before.

'I found out yesterday that Simon
Garner is ill and will not be able to
play on Saturday.'

Mr Jones was deliberately spooning out the news in small, tantalizing helpings to enjoy the effect it was having upon his young pupil. Chris's eyes were opening wide with the dawn of understanding.

Simon was the regular school team goalkeeper.

He could hardly wait for the next magic words as all fears of the witch were blown out of his mind.

'Well, I've thought very hard about it,' the headmaster smiled, 'and I've decided to pick you for your first match in goal for us.'

Chris tried to say something, but his throat tightened and he remained speechless.

'Congratulations! You're a very promising goalie, and I know you won't let us down.'

Chris was in too much of a shock to grasp anything else that was said, and he drifted back along the corridor to his classroom on a cloud.

'You're making it up!' Andrew exclaimed at morning break. 'He wouldn't risk picking a second year for a vital Cup game. We're playing Shenby School, our main rivals.'

Chris was a little hurt by his brother's outburst. Part of the thrill for him was being chosen to play in the same side as Andrew. He had not stopped to think that Andrew might view his unexpected selection in rather a different light.

Like most boys, Andrew had had to wait until his final year at the school before being considered good enough for a place in the team, and he now enjoyed the respect and sense of importance it gave him. The sudden news that his kid brother was pinching some of the glory was a bit hard to swallow all at once.

To his credit, however, he tried hard to hide his feelings and was big enough to accept the new situation and come to terms with it by the time the bell went. 'Don't worry,' he told Chris as they lined up. 'Us defenders will look after you. Shenby will have to get past me first to reach you.'

One person who would be sure to welcome his great news, Chris knew, was their grandad who was always their biggest football fan.

That evening, as usual, Grandad was leaning over the back garden wall of his stone cottage that looked across the village recreation ground, puffing contentedly on his curved pipe. Chris ran up to him, his face flushed with excitement.

'Well, what an honour!' Grandad

said proudly. 'What did I tell you?'

He nudged Chris gently on the arm with his elbow as he often did when giving a piece of good advice or encouragement. 'I said you'd be in the team before you reckoned. To me, you're better than that Simon already.'

Chris grinned sheepishly at such praise. 'I don't know, Grandad. Simon's a good keeper. He'll be back when he's well again, I expect. It's just for this one match.'

'You never know. This is your big chance. Take it, and show them how good you are. Mr Jones has thrown you in at the deep end to see whether you sink or swim.'

He used his pipe this time to give Chris an affectionate prod to stress his point. 'I reckon you'll swim all right.'

They looked over to where Andrew and some of his friends were kicking a ball about on the village team's pitch. The primary school had to use it too, as their own playing field was too small for proper matches.

Chris was comforted by the thought that Grandad would be here, close by, to boost his confidence on Saturday. He always watched his games lessons too and usually made helpful comments afterwards about his performance in goal.

'Try to learn from your mistakes,' was one of Grandad's favourite sayings. 'It might stop you giving away a similar goal in future.'

They chatted for a while longer

until Grandad said, 'You ought to go across and join in. It looks like they need a decent keeper and you need some extra practice. You're in training for the big match now, you know.'

He gave his grandson a wink to send him on his way and then smiled. He felt sure he was looking forward to Saturday almost as much as the lad himself!

3   In Training

'C'mon! Simon gobbles them up for breakfast,' came the stinging criticism as Chris fumbled a shot early in their kick-about. 'We'd better not get knocked out of the Cup because of you, or you've had it!'

The threat was made by Simon's best mate, John Duggan, too low for Andrew to hear, but forcibly enough to leave Chris in no doubt who would be blamed for any defeat, whether his fault or not.

He quickly realized that he could not win their respect merely because he was Andrew's brother. Two years or so difference in age was a wide gap to bridge, unless he could prove himself in their company. He knew he would have to earn recognition of his goalkeeping ability by his own efforts.

Soon afterwards Duggan was put clean through to goal from a brilliant pass by school team captain Tim Lawrence, and Chris immediately went out towards him to try and narrow the shooting angle.

The two of them were on collision course and Duggan drove in extra hard as Chris dived bravely down at his feet, catching him a painful blow on the shoulder with his right boot. Chris still managed to cling on to the ball, though, and struggled to his feet, rubbing the spot rather gingerly.

Andrew squared up angrily to John Duggan. 'That was a deliberate dirty foul!'

'Rubbish!' Duggan snarled back. 'He's got to toughen up and expect a few knocks if he wants to be a goalie.'

Andrew was fired up enough to want to take their argument further, but Tim stepped between them just in time to cool rising tempers.

'Go easy, Duggie, we don't want another keeper crocked.'

The forward turned away. 'Huh! It wouldn't matter. Somebody else could go in goal . . . somebody *older*.'

'There's nobody else better than our Chris,' Andrew blurted out. But then he checked himself, surprised at the strength of his support for his younger brother against one of his own group of friends. He was the only one allowed to insult Chris and get away with it!

'It's okay, Andrew,' Chris put in. 'Thanks for sticking up for me, but let's just get on with the football. I'm all right.'

There were a few more lingering glares, but the incident was put behind them in the general hurly-

burly of the game, which continued until the light began to fade.

'Let's pack up now — it's getting too dark,' Tim decided. 'Remember we've got our main practice here tomorrow after school.'

He went up to Chris. 'Well played. You made some good stops. You'll do for me.'

Chris was delighted to find the captain on his side and forgot about

the ache in his shoulder until their grandad asked about it before they went home.

'It's fine. Just a bit sore, that's all.'

Grandad nodded his approval. 'Good. You'll certainly get far worse cracks than that playing in goal. You know what the old saying is, don't you?'

'What's that?' Chris grinned, already guessing the reply.

'All goalkeepers are crazy! That's what they always say,' he chuckled, and knocked his pipe on the stone wall to empty out its charred remains.

The following afternoon the school soccer squad clattered across the footbridge over the river Dane, which wrapped itself around the recreation

ground on its rippling way through the village.

Mr Jones brought up the rear of the party and quickly organized the boys into small groups to practise their passing and ball control skills. He then took the new young keeper into the goalmouth with two others to help in order to give him some special individual attention.

Soon Chris was diving about in all directions as they kicked and threw balls at him at different speeds and heights. Some bounced awkwardly just in front of him while others had him stretching upwards to reach. All the time the headmaster encouraged him either to hold on to the ball or to push it right away to one side out of danger.

'Try to get some part of your body behind your hands if you can,' he told him. 'There's nothing worse than letting a ball slip through your fingers and then between your legs as well for a goal.'

He knew, though, that Chris had quite a safe pair of hands and usually positioned himself well to deal with most shots. Even so, when the ball was hit well above his mop of fair hair

he had little chance of stopping it in these goals, which were really too high and wide for boys of this age.

Taking a brief break from the coaching, Mr Jones exchanged a few words over the wall with the boy's grandad who was watching with great interest. 'Still got a lot to learn of course, young Chris, but he's coming on well. He's so keen.'

'Aye, he is that,' the old man

replied proudly. 'He'll make a fine keeper one day, you mark my words.'

The session included a vigorous seven-a-side game with everyone trying extra hard to impress in the hope of getting picked for the Cup match. Chris, in fact, did not have the happiest of times in this, and blamed himself for a couple of goals he let in, especially one by John Duggan.

He allowed the big lad's powerful challenge to distract him enough to take his eye off the ball for a vital second. He dropped it at Duggan's feet, allowing him to poke it over the unguarded line.

'Got you rattled, have I?' he jeered. 'That's no good. If Shenby find out you're a softie, they'll murder you!'

Chris ignored the unfair jibe and renewed his concentration on the

50

game, but he guessed Andrew had overheard. In the next attack the defender took revenge by crunching into Duggan — hard but cleanly — to win the ball just as he was about to try another shot.

Finally the headmaster gathered them together to give out further bits of advice and then announce the team.

'It should be a good close match,' he predicted before sending them

home, 'but win or lose, I hope you all enjoy it. It's the way you play that matters, remember, not the final result.'

The two brothers trailed off for their tea still full of talk about the coming game. The prospect of their playing together for the first time was now beginning to appeal to Andrew more and more. 'Duggie's okay, really,' he tried to explain. 'Once you get to know him. It's just that he hates to lose at anything, despite what old Jonesy always says.'

'Well, he's not exactly helping our chances by getting at me all the time,' Chris grumbled.

'Oh, forget it. He's like that with everyone. He's seen you make enough good saves to know you'll be all right.'

'That's the trouble. I hope I will. I'm getting scared about perhaps letting in a daft goal that costs us the match.'

Andrew laughed. 'You won't do anything like that. You'll play a blinder on Saturday. I mean, with you in goal and me in defence, Shenby don't stand a chance of scoring!'

Chris only wished it would be as easy as Andrew made it sound. But as it turned out, Andrew too had cause to regret his choice of words.

During the next two days at school Chris had little time for brooding about what might happen, as his class teacher worked him extra hard to prevent his thoughts from wandering too much on to football. But Chris didn't really mind. It was all worth it. He was soon going to wear that treasured green jersey.

At breaks he could hardly stay away from the sports notice-board. His eyes were drawn to the list of names for the Shenby match. It gave him a delicious tingle up and down his spine every time he saw written beside the goalkeeping position the

name . . . C. Weston.

He had to keep checking that it was still there. It was somehow proof that he had made it at last. Nothing could stop him from playing now. Nothing!

Except perhaps for a dramatic, unfortunate change in the weather . . .

4 *Kick-Off*

'Is it never going to stop?' Chris whined.

The two boys stared miserably out of their rain-spattered bedroom window.

'It's been raining for hours,' Andrew muttered. 'The match will be called off at this rate.'

Chris was appalled.

'Off! You mean, cancelled?'

His dreams began to disappear down the drain with all the rainwater.

'Could be. Pitch waterlogged, they call it.'

'It can't be!' Chris cried out. 'Simon'll be fit again then before I even get a chance to play.'

They looked at each other with equal dismay.

'C'mon, it'll probably be okay,' said Andrew more optimistically. 'No use worrying about it. Let's try and get some sleep.'

They lay in the darkened room, Chris too tense and nervous to close his eyes as he thought about Andrew's final words before he had switched off the light. 'If we do play tomorrow, it's sure going to be muddy. We'll be sliding about all over the place. Great!'

But the likelihood of a slippery ball

to handle was not helping Chris's peace of mind at all.

Suddenly he sat bolt upright in bed.

'Gloves!' he exclaimed loudly. 'Oh no! My goalie's gloves. I've left them at school.'

'You idiot!' came a weary reply from nearby. 'You're hopeless.'

'What can I do?'

'Nothing. They won't go and open up the school just for you, so you'll just have to manage without. Serves you right — it might improve your memory in future.'

Slowly, however, even the sleepy Andrew began to appreciate the possible serious consequences for the team. 'Haven't you got any others to wear?'

Chris shook his head. 'Only my

ordinary gloves. Mum would go mad if I messed them up.'

They considered the problem for several minutes until Chris let out a whoop.

'The witch's gloves!'

He scrambled out of bed and fished them out from the top drawer of his cabinet.

'I thought you'd already taken them into school for the jumble,' Andrew said.

'I kept forgetting,' Chris confessed, and then laughed. 'You see, it helps to have a bad memory sometimes!'

Andrew gave up and watched his brother pull them on.

'They're nice and rough so I'll be able to grip the ball okay, I reckon. Good old witchy! Hey! They might even have a lucky magic spell on them.'

'Fat chance of that,' Andrew scoffed. 'More likely to be unlucky, if you ask me. But I suppose they're better than nothing. How do they feel?'

'Ace! They fit like a glove!' Chris joked.

Andrew collapsed back on to his pillow with a groan and then decided to throw it at him to stop him prancing around the room.

After heavy overnight rain, the new day dawned grey and chilly, but a strong, gusty wind was helping to dry out some of the puddles of water lying in every hollow. The brothers ran all the way to the ground, desperate to find out whether the big match was still on or not, and arrived breathless to join a few others already there.

'Lovely and squelchy!' They heard Duggan's voice raised above the rest. 'Little Westy is going to be a real stick in the mud today.'

He was standing in the goalmouth as they approached, the mud oozing over the toes of his wellingtons. There were a few pools of brown water to be seen in the centre circle and both penalty areas, but the state of the pitch down the wings did not seem too bad.

'What do you reckon?' Andrew asked Tim Lawrence, who would have to plough through the mess in midfield more than most.

'Mr Jones told me he thought it was playable if there's no more rain,' Tim replied, 'but the final decision's up to the referee. He's inspecting the pitch now.'

'Are Shenby here yet?' Chris asked.

'Not yet,' Duggan interrupted quickly. 'Getting cold feet, are we?

'No. Just wondered, that's all,' he defended himself.

Even so, he could feel the butter-flies churning around inside his stomach with his hurried breakfast. He hated standing about waiting, and he was impatient for things to start happening.

At that moment Mr Jones came across to them. He tried to look as though he had bad news but couldn't keep his face straight as he saw the disappointment in their eyes. 'It's okay, lads,' he grinned at last, 'we're going ahead and hoping for the best.'

They let out a cheer of relief and he had to calm them down again before he could continue. 'It's bound to be tricky underfoot so keep it simple. No fancy stuff near your own goal in this mud. Get the ball away to safety.'

He looked at Chris uneasily. 'Not ideal conditions for your first game, I'm afraid, but good luck. Watch for the ball skidding about. And don't worry, whatever happens, nobody's going to grumble at you if you do make any mistakes.'

Chris shot a glance at the smirking Duggan and felt that this last remark was perhaps not strictly accurate.

'Have you got some gloves?' Mr Jones asked him.

He gulped and avoided Andrew's face. 'Yes,' he said simply.

'Good. You'll certainly be needing them today.'

As he spoke, a convoy of vehicles began to unload a cargo of eager Shenby footballers and Mr Jones went off to welcome them, leaving his own players to troop into the wooden changing hut. Chris felt a gentle nudge on the arm.

'All the best,' whispered Grandad into his ear, and Chris turned in delight. 'Keep your eye on the ball — the wind will be swirling it about this morning.'

'I will, Grandad.'

They grinned at each other and Chris felt reassured, but quickly he was swallowed up inside the noisy, excited atmosphere of the hut, as both teams hurriedly changed.

At last came the moment that he had dreamed of for ages. Mr Jones held out to him the school team goal-keeper's green top with the black figure 1 standing out on the back. The number 1 keeper in the world, he pretended it meant.

'A little earlier than I'd planned,' the headmaster smiled, 'but I'm sure you'll be seeing a lot more of it in time to come.'

The boy clutched his prize lovingly close to his chest as if to prove his dream had indeed come true. 'Thank you,' he murmured.

As soon as he pulled the jersey over his head all nervousness and doubt vanished. He was ready to face anybody. No matter how many more times he might wear it, he knew that he would never forget that first marvellous sensation of feeling its extra padded warmth against his bare skin.

Now he was a real goalkeeper!

He swiftly slipped into his white shorts, tugged on the red socks and laced his boots up tightly. Then, the witch's gloves in one hand, he clattered down the steps out on to the soft, spongy turf. Danebridge's red and white stripes mingled with Shenby's blue shirts as the two sides jogged towards the pitch to warm up. Their bright, freshly-washed kits were not destined to stay those colours for long, however, on such a mud-heap.

The new young goalkeeper spotted his grandad on the touchline giving him an encouraging thumbs-up signal. The importance of the occasion was reflected by the fact that his usual place behind the garden wall was not near enough

today to enjoy his grandson's performance to the full. Chris waved back and then returned the greetings from some of his own friends kicking a ball about just off the pitch.

The fleeting thought entered his head that normally he would have been there with them, playing their own little game and only half watching the main action, but still managing to raise a cheer when Danebridge scored a goal. Today, though, was very different. He knew they would have given anything to be able to swap places with him and actually play for the school team.

Chris forced himself to put them out of his mind and to concentrate on the job in hand. He saw that the goalmouth nearer the River Dane was in a far worse state than the other and realized that the wind was blowing towards it too. Not surprisingly, his spirits sagged a little when the Shenby captain won the toss and indicated he wanted to attack that way first in the hope of gaining an early advantage.

'Just my luck,' he muttered to himself.

Tim Lawrence, though, did not seem to mind. 'Suits us,' he called to his team, clapping his hands to urge them to play well. 'We'll have the wind behind us in the second half when they're tiring.'

He managed a quick word with Andrew. 'Keep the defence tight. We've somehow got to hold on till half-time. Try and give Chris an early feel of the ball, if you can, to settle him down.'

The referee blew his whistle and Chris stood alone in the swampy goal-mouth as the game at last kicked off, his face set with determination to do well.

But his soccer career was fated to get off to a disastrous start. By the time he did get his hands on the ball, Danebridge were already one goal

down in the most tragic manner and there was nothing that he could have done to prevent it.

In Shenby's very first attack, they swept the ball down the right touch-line to allow their winger to run at the home side's left-back. Normally the defender would have easily cut out the danger, but as he turned, his feet slithered from underneath him on the greasy surface and his opponent raced past him into the clear.

The winger dribbled into the penalty area and seemed to be trying to set himself up for a shot. Chris was correctly positioned at the near post to block it when, unexpectedly, the ball was hooked hard and low across the face of the goal.

Andrew had been hurtling in to

mark their centre-forward and had no chance to get out of the way of the speeding missile. It struck him on the left knee and flew off wickedly into the top corner of his own goal.

The brothers gaped at each other in horror as Shenby celebrated their lucky success. For Chris, it seemed as though time itself stood still. His feet felt so heavy he could not even move them.

Everything, somehow, faded far away and he felt very small and lonely. His dream-world had caved in around him and the prickle of salty tears stung behind his eyes.

Vaguely, a familiar yet strangely pathetic voice got through to him.

'Sorry, little brother,' he heard it apologize. 'I couldn't help it — honest.'

5 Penalty!

'Forget it, both of you. C'mon, we've got work to do.'

Tim had already fetched the ball and now ruffled Chris's hair to try and cheer him up. 'Nobody's fault,' he continued. 'Let's just get on with the game.'

Similar shouts of encouragement were now floating across from the people on the touchline, but Chris didn't want to look over to where Grandad was standing. He still felt so miserable.

He didn't have much time to gaze around anyway. All too quickly Shenby were threatening his goal again, but this attack broke down and Chris was able to gather up the loose ball and boot it away upfield to get rid of some of his frustration. His first touch had not been a very happy one.

Things almost worsened a minute later when the score nearly became 2-0 after he misjudged a shot completely. He thought he had it covered until the ball dipped in the wind, bounced awkwardly just in front of him and then squirmed through his fingers. With great relief, he saw it swerve to one side and clip the outside of the post instead of going in.

'Good job for you,' came Duggan's angry warning from nearby.

'Leave him alone,' Andrew challenged, 'and let him settle down. He'll be all right. You get back up front and score us a goal.'

'Seems like you're doing all the scoring round here,' Duggan taunted with a sneer, reminding him painfully of his own goal.

Shenby continued to press hard to try and increase their lead. His confidence shattered, Chris fumbled more shots and the whole defence caught his jitters as they panicked and miskicked their clearances.

Added to these troubles on the pitch, Chris became aware of other irritations behind his goal. A couple of older Shenby boys had wandered up and were now deliberately trying to put him off. Their first casual comments were soon followed by jeers and insults at his mistakes, and then they began to throw little chunks of mud in his direction when they thought no-one was looking.

But somebody was.

One piece caught Chris on the back of his neck. 'Pack it up,' he shouted, but that only made them laugh and do it even more. He was at a loss to know how to cope with the situation.

Help arrived, however, before matters got out of hand. Grandad did not normally like to interfere, but today was different. He decided to put a stop to their unfair and unsporting tactics.

'Right! No more of that nonsense, you two,' he announced firmly.

Startled by his sudden appearance

on the scene, the boys did not even attempt to run off and they found themselves being escorted round the pitch, without fuss, to be left in the charge of the Shenby teacher.

Grandad slipped Chris a wink on his way back. 'They won't be bothering you again this match.'

Chris nodded gratefully, and it was straight after this that he made his first decent save when he flung himself low to his right to smother a fierce drive.

That made him feel a whole lot better, and the thud of another shot into the front of his muddy green jersey signalled to his team that at last their keeper had found his form and they could breathe more easily. They had survived the crisis.

But there were still some heart-stopping moments inside the

Danebridge penalty area, as when one inswinging corner flopped into the goalmouth mud to cause a frantic scramble of legs, boots, arms and bodies. The ball cannoned about off players for what seemed like an age, and twice Chris blocked point-blank range efforts without being able to hang on to it. Finally, the confusion was ended when Andrew hacked it right off the line to clear the danger.

'Thanks!' cried Chris in the excitement. 'That makes up for earlier,'

His entire kit was filthy wet by now, but he became almost unrecognizable moments later when he landed full-length, face down, in the largest of the puddles. He stood up, still clutching the ball from his save, with his hair, face and body caked in dark, sticky mud, but grinning widely, his white teeth gleaming through all the dirt. He made a comical sight, but he was loving every minute of being in the thick of the action.

Shenby's pressure paid off, however, with a clever second goal and Chris could do nothing to prevent it. A tricky piece of skill from the left-winger allowed him to jink past two tackles and send an unstoppable shot high over the goalkeeper's head.

In smaller-sized, schoolboy goals it would undoubtedly have sailed over the crossbar as well, but in these it passed comfortably underneath.

There were no nets on the posts and Chris had to recover the ball from the hedge behind, but soon he was smiling again when he watched his opposite number make a similar trip. The visitors' goalkeeper had enjoyed a rather idle first half so far and was caught napping completely by a swift breakaway Danebridge raid seconds before the interval.

It was Tim Lawrence who popped up unmarked in the Shenby area to steer a cross coolly over the line to leave his team only 2-1 down, a well-deserved reward after so much hard work in defence.

Mr Jones was quick to praise everyone at half-time and give them further encouragement. 'The wind's in your favour now in the second half, remember, so go out and show them how to attack.'

He turned to Chris. 'Well played! You've done us proud after a shaky start. But keep on your guard still — it's not over yet.'

It was just as well that Chris did remain alert.

Straight after the re-start the big Shenby centre-forward burst clear for goal with only the keeper to beat. But as he tried to dribble past him, Chris pounced and spread himself down at his feet, grabbing the ball as the attacker sprawled forwards on top of him.

Enjoying the applause, Chris kicked the ball triumphantly away and his brave, important save inspired the whole Danebridge team to put together a series of skilful attacks of their own to prove that they could play good football too.

Even so, it took ten minutes before Shenby cracked, and then they conceded two quick goals.

The equalizer was scored by John

Duggan, challenging strongly as usual in a goalmouth scramble and forcing the ball over the line. Immediately afterwards, with Shenby's defence still disorganized, Tim set off on a thrilling solo run, showing superb balance on the slippery ground. Dancing round several tackles, he cut inside from the right and hit a beauty into the far corner beyond the keeper's desperate dive.

Danebridge suddenly found themselves 3—2 ahead and looked well set for victory.

'You've got 'em on the run now,' one of the fathers called from the touchline. 'Keep it up. Let's have more goals.'

But the boys on the pitch knew it was not as simple as that. Shenby were far from finished. They refused to give in, and in fact the shock of falling behind had seemed to put fresh life into them, as they now charged around in search of the equalizer which would earn them a replay at home.

The Cup match became an exciting end-to-end battle as the teams threw everything they had left at each other and both goals survived several narrow squeaks. Time was rapidly running out, though, for Shenby when they forced Chris to tip the ball round the post for yet another corner and Tim signalled everyone back into the penalty area to protect their slender lead.

The winger played a neat short-corner before whipping the ball across into the box through a great

ruck of bodies. It suddenly loomed up in front of the unsighted Duggan who reacted by blocking it with his hand in panic before a Shenby player could get at it.

As he booted it away, the Shenby team and their supporters were already loudly demanding a penalty for hand-ball and he slumped to the ground in distress.

'It was an accident, I didn't mean to,' he pleaded, shaking his head and failing to find any excuse for his stunned team-mates. 'I don't know why I did it — it just happened . . .'

The referee had no choice, however, but to award a penalty kick and all their hard work seemed to be wasted. Duggan's eyes were not the only ones to be fixed now on goalkeeper

Chris in the desperate hope that he could yet somehow rescue the situation.

John Duggan wished he had not said so many nasty things to him, but it was too late to make up for that now. At least the kid was a good keeper, he had to admit to himself in consolation.

Chris had certainly proved that today to everyone, whatever happened in these next few minutes.

He settled himself on the goal-line, surprised that he felt quite calm considering that everything was at stake and it all seemed to depend upon him. He had never faced a proper penalty like this before and he was not really sure what to expect. The goal around him looked massive and he stared instead at the leather ball, noticing all the dirty marks on it as it sat perched up on the muddy penalty spot a few metres directly in front of him.

The spectators grew hushed in anticipation of the duel, the final shoot-out, and some of the players grouped around the edge of the area hardly dared to watch as the Shenby captain prepared to run in to take the penalty.

Duggan stood, head bowed, hoping for a miracle.

Grandad removed the pipe from his mouth, moistened his lips with his tongue and said a little silent prayer.

Mr Jones wiped his hand nervously down his face as the suspense and tension mounted.

But they could do nothing more to help. It was simply all up to Chris.

He crouched on his toes, waiting. Something Grandad once said about saving penalties suddenly flashed into his head: 'Decide which way to dive and do it — don't be tricked into changing your mind.'

He rubbed his gloved hands together to scrape off some of the mud which clung to them, and then decided: he would go left. Somehow, he had to get in the way of it . . .

The whistle sounded in the silence, and the kicker moved confidently in.

Wham!

The ball was blasted hard and he dived, almost blindly, to his left. But too far!

His hunch had proved correct, but

the ball had been struck only just left of centre and he felt it smack against his legs.

Chris lay helpless on the ground as it rebounded off him and the screams from the crowd jerked everybody into action.

Duggan's head shot up to see the stranded keeper trying unsuccessfully to scramble to his feet in the slime and the penalty-taker flat out too. He had lost his footing as he kicked the ball and was too dazed at his miss to recover quickly enough.

The ball was spinning crazily right in front of the vacant goal, but it was Andrew who reached it a split second ahead of other lunging feet to whack it out of sight.

The whole Danebridge team mobbed the brothers in sheer delight as the cheers rang out from the touchline.

'I take it all back!' shouted Duggan with huge relief. 'Fantastic save, Westy. Simon wouldn't have smelt it!'

'Just lucky,' Chris tried to say modestly, but his new friend wouldn't accept that.

'Don't talk rubbish. It was magic! Thanks for getting me off the hook.

I'd never have heard the last of it if they'd scored.'

Chris certainly never heard the last of that save. It was talked about for the rest of the season and beyond.

They would probably have kept talking then if Mr Jones had not managed to get their minds back on the game. But for Shenby it had been a cruel blow. Their heads went down and they could not hide their disappointment. They now seemed resigned to defeat and were fortunate, in fact, not to concede another goal before the final whistle blew shortly afterwards.

The Danebridge players celebrated their passage into the next round of the Cup by exchanging the traditional three cheers with Shenby as they gathered together at the end.

'What a game! What a game!' Andrew kept yelling, as he and John Duggan lifted Chris up on to their shoulders to carry him off the field in honour.

As for Chris, he couldn't quite believe it was all happening to him. It seemed almost unreal. But one thing he was sure about. Magic spell or not, the witch's gloves would never see the jumble sale. He would keep them for himself as a souvenir, a secret reminder of this special day as the school team goalkeeper.

Grandad walked back behind the footballers towards the hut with Mr Jones, enjoying their obvious pleasure.

'Thanks for making a young boy

very happy . . . and an old man too,' he said with a chuckle, his eyes wet and shining.

'Not my doing,' the headmaster replied, reflecting the credit back on to Chris. 'He took his big chance with both hands today. He's a hero now. A muddy hero!'